For my beautiful boy, Isaac

I HAVE A DOG

(an inconvenient dog)

CHARLOTTE LANCE

ALLEN&UNWIN
SYDNEY • MELBOURNE • AUCKLAND • LONDON

I have a dog.

An inconvenient dog.

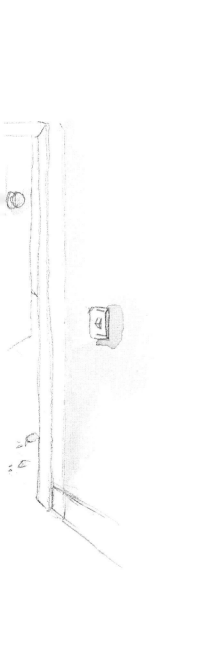

When I wake up,
my dog is inconvenient.

When I have breakfast,
my dog is inconvenient.

When I put my socks on,
my dog is inconvenient.

When I dig tunnels,

or when I want to play,

or build towers,
or read my books,

or go to the bathroom,
or play in the sandpit,
or try to put my toys away,
or wear my best shirt...

my dog is so INCONVENIENT.

But sometimes,

my dog is less inconvenient...

When I accidentally break something,

or I urgently need to fly,
my dog is less inconvenient.

When my dinner is disgusting,

or I watch something scary on TV,
my dog is less inconvenient.

And when at last it's time for bed,
my dog is always...

so convenient.

First published in 2014

Copyright © text and illustrations, Charlotte Lance 2014

Allen & Unwin
83 Alexander Street
Crows Nest NSW 2065
Australia
Phone: (61 2) 8425 0100
Email: info@allenandunwin.com
Web: www.allenandunwin.com

A Cataloguing-in-Publication entry is available
from the National Library of Australia
www.trove.nla.gov.au

ISBN 9 781 74331 781 5

Cover and text design by Sandra Nobes
Colour reproduction by Splitting Image, Clayton, Victoria

This book was printed in February 2014 at Hang Tai Printing (Guang Dong) Ltd.,
Xin Cheng Ind Est, Xie Gang Town, Dong Guan, Guang Dong Province, China.

1 3 5 7 9 10 8 6 4 2